ZEEKA AND THE ZOMBIES

BOOK I

REVENGE OF ZEEKA

AUTHOR BRENDA MOHAMMED

Contents

INTRODUCTION

How can one man use science for revenge?

ZEEKA AND THE ZOMBIES is the first story in the mind-blowing, multi-award-winning book Zeeka Chronicles.

The zika virus inspired the futuristic book series.

It's the year 2036, and it's a high-tech world.

Dr. Raynor Sharpe had a vision of zombie-like men with small heads walking on the beach. Was he dreaming, or was it a reality?

The woman he secretly loves, Janet Jones, is engaged to another man and is sleeping in the next room. Why is she there?

He received a call from Dr. George Brown of the Gosh hospital, where he works. Upon his arrival, he is surprised to hear Dr. Brown say that a zombie visited him. He said that he sedated him and placed him in Room Nine.

He had no name, and he called him Number Nine.

The zombie told Dr. Brown that his Master was Zeeka and there were fifty others like him planning an attack on the hospital.

The mystery deepens when Number Nine disappears from the hospital.

Was he really a zombie, and was he speaking the truth?

The plot thickens when Janet's wedding invitation reveals that her fiancé is Dr. Jason Stephens, whom the police suspect of being Master Zeeka.

Jason calls off the engagement with Janet and disappears.

Raynor finds Janet and finally proposes to her.

Did she accept?

Did the police find Zeeka?

Read a review from an ardent fan:

"This was such a fun read. The reading world is crammed with zombie stories, but I'll bet you haven't read one like this. It had the feel of an old black-and-white sci-fi movie, which I love, blended with modern themes and a more modern medical aspect.

Considering the length, I was surprised by how much was packed in it as things zipped along. I really loved Janet and Raynor, and found their relationship a nice addition. I'm so curious to learn more about the 'zombies' and Zeeka in the next parts."

I hope my readers will enjoy this fast-paced book.

RAYNOR HAS A VISION

The sound of sirens rudely awakened Raynor Sharpe from his bed. He seemed to hear screeching noises everywhere. Outside his house, people were screaming and shouting.

"What's all that commotion about?" he muttered. He tumbled off his bed, staggering and groping around for his eyeglasses. He could not find them in the confusion in the room. He looked around the room and searched amongst his clothes, which lay scattered on the floor. His eyes followed the bottle of wine and two wine glasses on the bedside table. He tripped on a woman's pair of red high-heeled shoes. "What the hell! Whose shoes are these? Did I have company last night?"

He could not recall what had happened the night before. As he looked around the room again, he saw female garments and underwear on the couch.

Half-asleep and puzzled, he scratched his head. "Was a woman here?" "Where are my glasses?" he shouted as he brushed aside clothing lying on the dressing table. His eyeglasses fell to the highly polished floor. He picked it up, put it on, pulled the curtain aside, and looked out of the window.

Am I awake? He shook his head as if to shake off his drowsiness. Is this something out of a science fiction movie? Am I seeing hundreds of short people with tiny heads walking like robots on the beach? He scratched his head again and then pinched himself. That hurt. I am not dreaming.

He looked at the digital calendar on the wall to recall the date. It was Sunday, 30th January 2036. He flung open the window to take another look at the beach. The pungent smell of rotting fish invaded the room. He could hear the waves pounding on the seashore. There was no one in sight except a lone angler trying to pull in a catch. He wondered, did I have a vision? Where are the short, robot-like people? What about those noises I heard?

The visual telephone rang with a piercing sound. As he turned around to answer it, a woman walked out of the second bedroom. "J - Janet," he gasped, "You slept here last night?"

Janet stood there smiling. “Don’t you remember anything?”

She continued looking at him intently. He glanced up and down her beautiful, slim body. Her dark brown hair fell on her tanned shoulders.

“You mean we spent the night together?”

Janet laughed. “No, silly. I brought you home last night. You had too much to drink at the mayor’s ball. You’ve a lovely house here on the beachfront. I like it here.”

Raynor felt foolish. The phone continued to ring with a deafening sound. “Thanks, Janet. Did you tuck me into my bed?”

Janet pointed to the phone. “I only removed your shoes and jacket. Answer the phone.”

Raynor looked at the telephone, shaped like a small robot, and blurted out, “Hello.” There was a dial tone and no face at the other end. Whoever had rung had disconnected the call.

“There’s no one there. Probably a prankster called. Where’s my car? If you drove me home, where did I leave it?”

Janet shook her head and smiled. “You’ve forgotten, haven’t you? You left it at the hospital.

Dr. Mark Schmidt took you to the ball after you saw your last patient last night.”

Janet started walking around the house and stepped up to the window to admire the view. Raynor followed her and asked, “Did you see what I saw?”

Janet turned around to face Raynor. “What did you see?”

“The short people with small heads. Didn’t you see them?”

Janet laughed again. “There is no one out there, Raynor. You must have been dreaming.”

Raynor walked away from the window. “I swear I must have been wide awake. There were hundreds of people with small heads walking out there. I heard police sirens and people shouting and screaming.”

Janet glanced out the window a second time. “Looks awfully quiet to me. You probably have a hangover.”

Raynor murmured with a sigh of relief, "Maybe I dreamt it."

Janet was eager to change the conversation. "Let's have breakfast. I made you toast, scrambled eggs, and hot coffee."

Raynor seemed surprised. "Janet, you have worked at the hospital all these years, and you have helped me tremendously with my medical practice. You did not have to make me breakfast, too."

Janet started walking towards the kitchen and beckoned to Raynor to follow her. "I wanted to do it. I always start the day with a good breakfast. Let's enjoy it."

Raynor followed Janet to the kitchen and sat on the barstools. She had laid out the toast, bread, and coffee on the bar counter. A homely scent permeated the kitchen area. The aroma of freshly brewed coffee covered up the smell of the rotten fish.

He looked at her and thought, *I never dared to propose to her. I'm secretly in love with her all these years. I even purchased a diamond engagement ring, but kept it in my locker waiting for the right time.*

She's a ravishing beauty, especially without her doctor's coat. I wish I could have breakfast with her every morning for the rest of my life.

Raynor gazed at Janet. Her body curved in all the right places. She wore a soft red polka-dot dress. Her dark brown smiling eyes glanced at him. Her full lips had a slight pout like a younger version of Angelina Jolie. He kept staring at her as she sipped her coffee graciously.

Raynor was unaware that Janet was also eying him. She was thinking, *Raynor Sharpe is not a bad-looking person at all. In fact, he's very good-looking. He looks like my favorite movie star, George Clooney, in his younger days. He has great abs, too. I wonder why he never got married.*

Silence reigned in the kitchen as they ate breakfast. Both were engrossed in thoughts of their own.

Raynor Sharpe and Janet Jones worked at the Gosh Central Hospital. They were gynecologists and were amongst the best-known doctors on the island of Gosh. Janet had specialized in oncology and helped many cancer patients survive with a new drug that she had recently invented.

Raynor broke the silence, “This meal is delicious. Where did you learn to cook?”

Janet was pleased that Raynor was enjoying her cooking.

“Thanks. I’m glad you like it. My Mom taught me how to cook.”

Raynor built up the courage to ask Janet the next question. “Do you have a boyfriend?”

Janet dropped her fork on her plate and sat upright. “I thought you knew.

I’m engaged and will be getting married in the next two months.”

Disappointed in her reply he asked, “Who’s the lucky guy?”

Janet looked down at the floor. She seemed to be avoiding his eyes. “He’s a doctor too.”

Raynor could not stand the thought of Janet marrying someone else. He did his best to keep his composure. “Do I know him?”
Janet picked up her fork again and played with the food on her plate before she answered. “I doubt that very much. He works in another city. He does not attend many functions with me. He’s a very private person.”

After a brief interval, Raynor asked, “What’s his name?” Before she could answer, the shrill ringing of the phone interrupted their conversation. Raynor got up and walked swiftly over to the phone in the living area. Dr. Brown’s face appeared. “Good Morning, Raynor. Can you come over to the hospital right away? We need all the doctors we have on this case.”

“What’s wrong?” Raynor asked. “Who is it?” “Just get over here as fast as you can,” said Dr. Brown with a worried look on his face.

Raynor replied, “Sure, I’m on my way.” As he disconnected the call, he called out to Janet. “Get dressed quickly, Janet. The hospital needs us. You will have to drive me there since you said that my car is at the hospital.”

Janet jumped off the stool and headed for the bedroom to get dressed. “No problem,” she replied. As they got into the car, Raynor told Janet that Dr. George Brown, the Medical Chief of Staff from the hospital, had called. He wanted to see them on an urgent matter.

Janet’s car whizzed through the well-developed and prosperous little scenic island of Gosh off the coast of South America. Tourists from all over the world flocked that island for its well-known fabulous beaches and resorts.

Many were already there to attend the annual Carnival celebrations known internationally as the greatest show on earth. Despite its dark elements people did not want to miss the explosion of colour, music, revelry, and creativity. Tourists were seen along the streets with shopping bags as Janet and Raynor sped by.

Despite the presence of heavy police security, there were instances of serious crime occurring during the Carnival celebrations.

Notwithstanding new developments in technology and medicine over the past twenty years, the crime detection rate in the island had not improved much because of corrupt officers on the police force.

UNBELIEVABLE ENCOUNTER

When Raynor and Janet arrived at the hospital, all twenty doctors had gathered in the conference room. Dr. Mark Schmidt, a tall and strikingly dark and handsome man, walked over to Raynor and whispered in his ear, "Sorry, I could not take you home last night. I had an emergency. So glad that Janet agreed to do so."

Raynor nudged Mark and said, "No worries, Mark. Janet took good care of me."

Mark with a shocked expression replied, "But isn't she engaged to be married?"

Raynor laughed. "It's not what you are thinking. We're just friends."

Dr. George Brown, Chief of staff, walked into the room.

He was tall and slim, with graying hair. He was badly in need of a trim. He looked exhausted. He got right down to the purpose of the meeting by saying, "Thanks to all of you for turning up at such short notice. We have a problem.

In fact, we have an unbelievable problem. What I am about to tell you is to be kept strictly confidential until we decide if it will be necessary to bring in external help."

Dr. Brown gained the doctors' full attention with that opening remark. There was absolute silence for a few moments. If someone had dropped a pin on the floor, everyone would have heard the sound.

He continued. "A few of you may or may not have known that twenty years ago, the island of Gosh had an outbreak of a dreaded virus. The carrier was the Anopheles mosquito, a pest in Central and South America. Our island of Gosh is just off the coast of South America, and our people were vulnerable to that disease.

The virus had a debilitating effect on pregnant women and their babies. More than one hundred pregnant women were infected, and at the end of their full term, they gave birth to children at this hospital with small heads and little brain cells. They were all stillborn.

For safety and health reasons, the hospital did not give the dead babies to their parents for burial. The Government agreed to bury the children in separate graves in a vacant lot two miles from this hospital.

The hospital and Government took special care during burial to avoid contamination with the public. No funerals were held. Doctors who assisted in the delivery of the babies were Mark Schmidt and Raynor Sharpe, and they will recall these events.

We did not divulge any of this to doctors who joined the hospital after this had occurred."

Raynor's hand shot up in the air to attract Dr. Brown's attention.

Dr. Brown waved to him to put his hand down and went on speaking.

"You all will be shocked to hear what I'm going to tell you next."

He hesitated and looked around to make sure that the doors to the conference room were closed. "One of these babies, who we believe died and had been buried, is now a grown man, although short in stature. He is now in the Observation Unit under heavy sedation."

There was a loud uproar from the doctors. Raynor Sharpe stood up and shouted, "Dr. Brown, how could this be?" Dr. Brown replied,

“Please calm yourselves and listen to me. He walked into the hospital yesterday and came directly to my office and revealed the whole conspiracy. He claimed that there are fifty like him and they are zombies.”

There were shouts of “Unbelievable!” from almost all the doctors. Many just stared in disbelief.

Raynor recalled his vision that morning. “You say that he’s short and is a zombie. Is he healthy and of sound mind?” asked Dr. Raynor Sharpe.

Dr. Brown answered Raynor’s question. “He spoke well enough and looked like an average person, but he was wearing a false head. That head had electrical gadgets. I recorded everything he told me on my smartwatch before I removed that fake head and sedated him. He said his Master was Zeeka,

From what he said to me, this could be the work of a mad genius with evil intentions. I am going to play the recording for you now. It is a bit muffled. Please pay close attention.”

Dr. Brown turned on his smartwatch, and the doctors listened closely to the recording:

Number Nine:

“My name is Number Nine, and I grew up in an incubator with fifty others like me. We all have false heads and mechanical bodies. Our master tells us what to do by controlling the gadgets in our fake heads. He wants me and my brothers, to do evil things, and I am not bad. He calls us zombies and trains us to kill.”

Dr. Brown:

“Who is your Master?”

Number Nine:

“He said to call him Master Zeeka.”

Dr. Brown:

“Is Master Zeeka a doctor?”

Number Nine:

“He said that he is a great Scientist, and he saved us from the grave. He stated that although we were stillborn, he bribed a Government official to give him our bodies. He brought us back to life with a unique formula that only he knows. He kept us in incubators until we grew up. He then fitted our bodies with mechanical and electrical components.

Dr. Brown:

“Do you know where you live?”

Number Nine:

“I can show you, but that would be dangerous.”

Dr. Brown:

“Why is it dangerous?”

Number Nine:

“Because Master Zeeka said that he would kill anyone who disturbed his operation. He has many guards at the hideout. It is underground. Besides, we all are scientifically programmed to kill humans.”

Dr. Brown:

“So how did you escape from the hideout?”

At that point, Dr. Brown turned off the recording and said to the group of unbelieving doctors. “If any of these scientifically created men come to this hospital, please call Security right away and contact me.

We will remove their false heads and sedate them to prevent them from harming staff and patients. Please remember what I said earlier. We must keep this information confidential, even from our spouses, to avoid an island-wide panic."

Dr. Raynor Sharpe stood up again and said, "Sir, why did you turn off the recorder before we heard the answer to the last question?"

Dr. Brown replied, "Raynor I need to see you and Mark in my office right away." After saying that he walked hurriedly to his office.

Inside the conference room, the other doctors gathered in groups discussing the contents of the recording. They were debating whether Number Nine was indeed a zombie or a prankster.

The argument was that zombies display symptoms such as lethargic movement, language dysfunction, amnesia, and the inability to suppress hunger and aggression.

Doctors felt that the voice on the recording sounded like a normal human being, and if a zombie had the ability to speak, he could not be a zombie. One doctor believed that the false head, which was fitted with electrical gadgets, could have been wired to make the zombie sound like a human. They found it strange that he did not attack anyone or had a desire to eat human flesh. It was puzzling.

WAS IT A ZOMBIE?

"Sit down," Dr. Brown said to both doctors. "Now I will play the rest of the recording. Listen carefully." He then switched on the recorder on his smartwatch.

Dr. Brown:

"How did you escape from the hideout?"

Number Nine:

"I did not escape. Master Zeeka sent me here to spy on you and your hospital and report back to him with a plan to invade the hospital. He said when the virus became an epidemic he had created a vaccine to save all babies in their mothers' wombs, but you and other doctors were against it.

He said that you advised the Health Minister not to distribute the vaccine, and you condemned all babies conceived at that time to death. He stated that his mission is revenge."

"That is the end of the conversation. I was unsure if I could trust him so I removed his false head and sedated him. No one else has seen him. He is in Room 9 coincidentally.

Does either of you remember Dr. Jason Stephens? He is the scientist who invented the vaccine. Could he be Master Zeeka?" Dr. Brown asked.

Raynor began to feel sick in his stomach. The vision he had that morning kept recurring in his mind. Did he have a premonition? He spoke.

"I was wondering the same thing. We would have to find Dr. Stephens and the other fifty zombies at any cost. Should we get the police involved?"

Dr. Brown hesitated before he replied. "Can we trust anyone on the force? Do you know anyone who is not corrupt?"

Raynor looked at Mark for an answer and then suddenly remembered someone. "I was thinking of Detective Jack Wildy. He has an excellent reputation for solving crimes."

Mark responded, "I agree. Wildy is sharp."

Dr. Brown seemed to agree and said, "All right. Let's contact Wildy."

Raynor said, "I'll do that. First, can we have a look at Number Nine?"

Mark got off from his seat and said, "Yes, I want to see how that zombie looks. His voice does not sound like a zombie's."

Dr. Brown stood up and stretched out his arms and said, "This has been a burden on my mind since yesterday. I deliberated a lot before telling you all about it, but I knew that I could not keep it a secret. Let's go visit the zombie."

They walked down the long hallway to room nine, and Dr. Brown slowly opened the door. There was no one in there.

"What the heck is going on here?" shouted Dr. Brown who was visibly infuriated.

He ran down the hallway to press the alarm button. "Where are the guards?"

Mark and Raynor stood speechless in the room gazing at the empty bed which appeared to be neatly made up as if no one was ever there. They looked at each other.

Raynor said to Mark, "Do you know I had a vision this morning? I thought I saw hundreds of short people with small heads walking like robots along the beach in front of my home. Janet did not see them, and she said I must have been dreaming. I better call Detective Jack Wildy now."

Mark replied, "Yeah, do that. This whole thing is bizarre. I don't know what to think."

Dr. Brown returned to his office swearing. He looked exasperated. Several hospital staff members, who were all talking at once, followed him but did not enter his office.

Each one was trying to figure out how Number Nine escaped.

Dr. Brown said, "The false head is also gone. He must have put it on before he left. He would have looked like a typical male when he left the building."

Raynor and Mark knew Dr. Brown much longer than the other doctors did, and they called each other by their first names except in front of patients or junior doctors. Seeing him in a pensive mood, Raynor spoke in a low voice to him. "George, I contacted Jack Wildy. He is on his way with a team."

"Thanks, Raynor," he replied, looking half-dazed as he plopped down on his chair and looked out the window. Raynor noticed the glum look on his face, and went and sat next to him. "Could you remind me of the events of that virus outbreak twenty years ago?"

By that time, Dr. Brown had calmed down sufficiently to answer Raynor.

He swung around in his chair to face him. After letting out a deep sigh, he said, "The outbreak of the zika virus occurred when a group of nationals attended a conference in a neighbouring South American country where the virus was prevalent. Not all of them caught the virus, which in itself was no threat to life. When they returned to Gosh, those who had it transmitted the virus to their spouses by sexual contact.

Others contracted it through the spread of bacteria by sneezing and coughing by those individuals in public places during the weeklong annual Carnival celebrations in 2016. Before long, it had become an epidemic in the small island.

The primary danger was to the foetuses of pregnant women. Babies could have been born with unusually small heads that caused mental retardation and other developmental problems. Women were advised to avoid getting pregnant at that time, but many did not take that advice.

Dr. Jason Stephens was in charge of Scientific Research at the hospital at that point, and he had suspected a relationship between the virus and microcephaly.

Microcephaly is a rare neurological condition in which an infant's head is significantly smaller than the heads of other children of the same age and sex. He was unable to confirm that. He claimed to have created a vaccine to prevent microcephaly from affecting the foetuses, but the vaccine would have been life-threatening to the mothers.

I felt that the mothers' lives should have been the top priority and I was against using the vaccine. I advised the Health Minister accordingly. Dr. Jason Stephens and I had a heated argument over the matter, and he resigned from the hospital in a rage."

"It all sounds very familiar," said Raynor. "I do remember all of it now."

JACK WILDY INVESTIGATES

The stern voice of Detective Jack Wildy interrupted their conversation, and they both turned around to look at him. Jack Wildy looked as if he had just walked out of a detective novel. He seemed like the typical detective with a thick moustache and big ears. He was tall, dark, burly, dressed in stiff khakis, and a police officer's hat. He had a no-nonsense air about him.

He greeted Dr. Brown with these words, "Hi, Doc, I got Raynor's message. He said that you have a problem here." George was unsure if Jack would believe him. Besides, all he had was the recording on his smartwatch with a strange voice and his. How could he prove that Number Nine was real? No one else had seen him.

"Good Morning. Jack. Have a seat", he said. "What did Raynor tell you?"

Jack sat down, crossed his legs and replied, "He said that a strange guy came to see you and gave you a cock and bull story."

Raynor intervened, “No, we do not think it was a cock and bull story.”

Jack laughed out raucously. “I was joking. This matter sounds serious. Can I hear the recording?” He pulled out a pack of unusually long cigarettes and rocked back on the chair.

“Smoking in the hospital is not allowed, Jack,” said George as he was about to turn on his smartwatch. Jack put back the cigarettes in his pocket and sighed. ”Let’s listen to the recording, Doc.”

George turned on the recorder in the smartwatch. Jack took notes on his tablet as he listened to every word, but he also recorded the conversation on his smartwatch.

At the end of the recording, he laughed and said to George, “This guy is too smart to be a zombie. Is this all the evidence? I understand that he disappeared from the hospital. Do you realize that the police have nothing to work with except for voices on this recording? I suppose you do not even know where this so-called hideout is. Is he really a zombie? Did you do any blood tests on him?”

George was annoyed with Jack’s casual approach to such a serious matter. He answered him in a gruff manner. "Jack, I sedated him until we decided what we will do with him. I did not count on him leaving the hospital without our knowledge. And no, I do not know where the hideout is."

"All is not lost, Dr. Brown. I remember the zika virus outbreak. Raynor told me about Dr. Jason Stephens. It was all over the newspapers twenty years ago. Maybe that is why Dr. Stephens calls himself Master Zeeka. When I go back to my office, I will listen to the recording again and research Jason Stephens."

Jack rose from his chair. "I will leave now. Have a great day guys, and watch out for zombies. They may eat your flesh," he joked, as he walked away waving a hand behind his head. He turned around again briefly to say, "The government has drones everywhere and can see through walls even. This criminal will be caught."

Mark walked in just as Jack was leaving. "What did Jack say, guys?" Dr. Brown was in no mood to answer Mark. Raynor replied, "We have no evidence, and he has nothing with which to work. He is going to do research on Dr. Jason Stephens."

Mark seemed puzzled. “So what about the recording?” he asked.

“He said that only voices are on the recording,” George replied looking forlorn.

“There must be something that we can find out,” said Mark. “We’ll have to work together on this.”

George became serious. “Yes. We sure will. Right now, the hospital needs us. Let’s look after our patients.”

All three agreed. “I’ll begin my hospital rounds now,” said Mark.

“I’ll check the waiting area on my tablet and see if any patients are waiting for me,” said Raynor.

When Raynor returned to his office, Janet was sitting at his desk writing something. She looked up as he walked in and said, “I’m handing these out today. They are my wedding invitations. Remember I told you my wedding is in the next two months?”

Raynor forced a smile. “Oh yes, you did. What date is the wedding?”

With her right hand outstretched holding the invitation, she said, "March 30th is the big day. I hope you'll be there."

Raynor took the envelope, placed it in his desk drawer without reading it, and said, "Thanks. I hope I remember."

Janet stood up and said, "You better do, Raynor, or I'll be very upset. I have to deliver a couple more to other doctors, so I'll see you." She started to walk out of the office, then turned around and said, "Raynor, what do you make of that meeting with Dr. Brown? The voice on the recording sounded like an ordinary man, and then he disappeared. Doesn't the whole thing look fake?"

Raynor looked at her questioningly. He asked, "Is that what all the other doctors thought?"

She tossed her head to one side and replied, "Maybe." She then walked away.

Raynor sat at his desk and pondered over the events of the past few hours. George was around twenty years ago and witnessed the events. He believed him. It did not matter to him if others thought that George had come up with a fake story. He planned to get to the bottom of it, particularly, as he did not believe it was coincidental that he had such a strange vision that morning.

A hologram appeared with a nurse's face. Her voice brought him back to reality, "Dr. Sharpe to the maternity ward. It's an emergency."

Raynor, Mark, and George went back to their usual routine. Raynor and Mark were busy delivering babies and looking after patients, and George became tied up with the hospital administration and his patients. They had no time for chatting or discussing the events of earlier in the day.

After a long and hard day, Raynor drove home and fixed himself a TV dinner. He then fell fast asleep on the living room couch. He jumped up in the middle of the night, muttering, "Why do I keep dreaming this?" He had the exact dream as the night before.

He wanted to call Mark, but when he checked the time, he figured it was too late.

WHO IS MASTER ZEEKA?

The following morning at the hospital, Raynor went to Mark's office and told him about his dream. Raynor said that he had dreamt of an army of zombies marching towards the hospital. Mark stated that he should not take the dream seriously, but Raynor told him, "That dream is making my wish stronger to find that hideout."

"How are you going to do that?" asked Mark with raised eyebrows. An idea suddenly struck Mark. "Let's look up the telephone listings for Jason Stephens."

Raynor jumped off his chair. "That's a good start, Mark. Why didn't I think of that?"

Mark turned on the digital directory on his desk and looked under S for Stephens.

There were lots of Stephens but no Jason Stephens. "We've reached a dead end here. I'll think of something else, but right now, I have to see my patients. I'll talk to you later," Mark told him.

Raynor nodded his head and went back to his office feeling frustrated.

Meanwhile, Number Nine had returned to the hideout and was discussing with Master Zeeka his meeting with Dr. Brown.

“So tell me about your little adventure,” Master Zeeka said to Number Nine.

“I gained Dr. Brown’s confidence, but then he removed my false head and tried to sedate me,” said Number Nine.

“I mapped out a plan of the hospital in my mind when he thought that I was asleep. You can download it.”

“Ha! Ha! He does not know that their sedatives cannot work on you or any of my creations. Only that headpiece with its gadgets which I control with this little device can cause you to take action,” Master Zeeka said, waving a device with dozens of buttons on it.” You and your companions can only do my bidding because I control your minds from this instrument. It is a transponder. I am the greatest scientist that man has ever known. Do you agree?”

“Of course, Master. You are the best,” said Number Nine.” I overheard doctors arguing and saying that we zombies like human flesh.

Why is it that I do not want to eat human flesh?"

"I did not program any of you to feed on human flesh. I programmed you to eat certain foods, but no human flesh whatsoever," Zeeka said.

"Why not human flesh?" Number Nine asked him.

"Because human flesh weakens your body. When I brought back all fifty-one of you from the grave, I injected each of you with a serum that resists meat.

It's the only way to keep me alive and perform my experiments," Zeeka replied.

"Keep you alive? What does that mean?" asked Number Nine.

"Because if I did not inject you all with that serum to remove the will to eat human flesh, you all would have fed on me. Do you understand?"

"I get it," said Number Nine.

"You're very smart. Let me borrow your head so that I can download that map to my secret files," said Zeeka.

"Your companions are all resting. I have their heads in my locker. You can rest too. Soon it will be Carnival, and we have to continue practicing for that great national event. So rest a lot. We'll have another practice session later."

Zeeka then removed Number Nine's head and switched it to 'No activity.' Number Nine fell back in a lifeless mode, and Zeeka took him into the room with the other zombies to rest.

At the hospital, Raynor had just delivered a baby. He went to his office to update the records.

Janet was passing to visit a patient in the oncology centre, and she called out to him. "Hey, Raynor, have you read the invitation yet? I want you to RSVP as soon as possible so that I can finalize the catering."

"Ah," he sighed. "I will do that soon. I promise. Nevertheless, you can count me in as I'll not miss your wedding for the world."

"I was hoping that you would say that. Bye for now."

WAS IT JUST A SILLY DREAM?

A couple of weeks went by, and Dr. George Brown could not get over the embarrassment he faced when Number Nine disappeared from the hospital. He played the recording of their conversation repeatedly trying to get clues but came up with nothing. Raynor and Mark did not speak about it either.

Detective Jack Wildy did not call to say that he got anywhere with the investigation. Could it have been just a silly dream? He opened his desk drawer with the 'open' button and saw Janet's wedding invitation lying in there. He never had time to read it. He was just about to open it when Raynor walked into his office.

"How are you today, sir?" asked Raynor as he pulled up a chair to sit.

"I'm fine, Raynor. What's on your mind? I'm happy that you stopped by to see me."

"I cannot get that recording off my mind. It worries me that we suspect who may be behind all of this and we are helpless to do anything about it," replied Raynor.

"So you do believe me. What about Mark? Does he feel the same way?"

"We both believe you. We want to get to the bottom of this, but we also need outside help."

"Did you hear from Jack Wildy?" asked Dr. Brown.

"He has not called since he heard the recording. Do you want me to follow up with him?"

"I suppose it would not hurt to try. We have to be very careful. I feel as if a bomb is waiting to explode. I'm not sure if we can trust anyone," Dr. Brown cautioned.

There was a knock on the door. It was Mark. "What's up, guys? Any news on Number Nine?"

"No news is good news, and in this case, we have no news. We have not found out his whereabouts or his Master's location. What's up with you?" asked Dr. Brown.

"Well, maybe they may expose themselves during the Carnival celebrations next week. We have to be on the alert. It is important that Detective Wildy gets involved," said Mark.

"There'll be chaos if they appear at Carnival. Raynor was just saying that he is going to contact Jack Wildy again." When is Carnival?"

"Carnival is taking place next week," said Raynor. "We don't have much time. I'm going to meet Jack right now."

"Haven't you and Mark found it strange that Nine can speak and he understood what I was asking him?

Jack was right. He is too smart to be a zombie."

"That's indeed strange. This person is a mystery. I'd love to meet him," Raynor said, getting up to leave. Both Mark and Dr. Brown wished him good luck.

When Raynor arrived at Jack's office, he saw him with a pile of old newspapers on his desk. "Good day Jack. I dropped in to find out if you made any headway into that investigation you promised to look into for us."

"Sit, Raynor. Do you want a cup of coffee?" Jack stood up to pour a cup of coffee from the Coffee Dispenser.

"I'll have one. Thanks, Jack."

Jack poured two cups of coffee, handed one to Raynor and sat down next to him. "I've not forgotten about the investigation. I was waiting to get real facts before I contacted you and Dr. Brown. I've dug up these newspapers from the archives, as I can find nothing of substance in the computer records.

Look at this article and the picture of Dr. Jason Stephens. Dr. Brown thinks he is our suspect."

"I remember him well. He's sharp-looking. I wonder if his hair is still black or has turned gray," said Raynor, looking at the headline on the article, which read, "Scientist discovers a vaccine for the dangerous Zika virus."

"So you know this guy? I lived in America twenty years ago. I never knew about him until now," said Jack. "Do you know he resembles you?"

Raynor looked at the photo again, and after carefully examining it, he shrugged his shoulders and said, "Maybe he does. Do you think he is Master Zeeka? Do you think that he scientifically created fifty-one zombies from those dead babies? Is this at all possible?"

Jack replied, "Anything is possible. There was a similar case in Africa years ago. The police discovered their hiding place after it was burnt to the ground.

The scientist was killed in the fire, but his records mysteriously disappeared from the fire-proof safe."

"Dr. Brown and Dr. Schmidt both believe that these zombies will create havoc during the Carnival celebrations. We must stop that from happening," said Raynor.

"We'll be monitoring the celebrations carefully. I have already discussed with the Chief of Police the possibility of zombies making an appearance."

"Are you saying that the Chief of Police is also on the case?" Raynor asked in amazement.

"Oh, yes. I spoke to him, and he considers this high priority," said Jack.

"That's good news," said Raynor. "Can we all relax now?"

"Just be alert and give me all information if you find out anything," Jack replied.

"I will. I will," repeated Raynor as he stood up to leave.

MASSACRE AT CARNIVAL

The first day of the Carnival celebrations started with a fantastic display of bands.

Janet, her mother, and two sisters were in the north stands of the Carnival Arena enjoying the parade of bands, which started at 9.00 am. The weather was just right. It was not very hot; neither was it cold. It was quite comfortable. The colourful costumes delighted the thousands of nationals and tourists who filled the stands. The steel band music was tantalizing, and the atmosphere was just incredible.

Several groups crossed the stage with hundreds of young girls and men wearing skimpy but stunning costumes, decorated with colourful feathers, sparkling beads, and glitter.

Just before noon, a small sailor band pulling a lovely decorated boat came on stage. The sailors were all the same height and size and dressed in magnificent, fur-trimmed, colourful, embroidered, and embellished sailor suits with oversized hats of similar material. They were dancing and prancing on the stage and pulling the boat along the stage. They then stopped in the middle of the stage to do antics. They took off their hats and waved them to the crowd. The crowds loved it and started cheering loudly.

The applause encouraged them to do more antics, and they continued throwing around their hats and dancing to the beat of the steel band music. In the middle of all the fun, Janet's mother started to feel hungry and asked Janet to get her something to eat. Janet dutifully went to the back of the arena to buy food for her Mom and sisters.

She walked around the various food stalls manned by robotic waiters to see what they were selling. She decided that her Mom and sisters would love to indulge in a Carnival chicken dish. She bought four meals. As she turned around to return to the stands, she heard gunfire and loud explosions. She observed bullets were flying from the sailors' heads, and that seemed odd. People were screaming and falling to the ground.

Blood was splattered everywhere. Those who were not injured or killed were tumbling over each other to get out of the Arena. The Emergency alarm went off, and police sirens started blaring as police cars and helicopters encircled the area within minutes.

The police aimed at the attackers on stage and rapidly fired on them until every one of them fell to the ground. Janet, concerned for the safety of her Mom and sisters as well as the spectators, dropped the food boxes to the ground and pushed her way through the crowd.

She kept shouting, "I'm a doctor. Let me through, please." When she arrived at the spot where she had left her mother and sisters, she saw them huddled on the ground hugging each other.

"Are you hurt?" she asked.

"No Janet we are fine, but look on the stage." Janet turned towards the stage and could not believe her eyes. The bodies of the sailors and the boat had disintegrated into black ash in a few seconds. Not a trace of a body remained. "How's that possible?" said Janet.

Many patrons were lying dead in pools of blood. Severed arms and legs dripping with blood were strewn about the stands. The injured and bleeding needed urgent transportation to the hospital for treatment.

She said to her Mom and sisters, “Can you find your way home? Duty calls.”

Her Mom replied, “We understand, dear. Do not worry about us.”

She took out her transmission phone from her handbag and called the hospital to send all the ambulances available to the Carnival Arena. Within seconds, ambulances arrived with the necessary personnel to take the seriously injured to the hospital. Morgue attendants came too and collected the dead bodies and severed arms and legs in body bags to take to the mortuary.

At that moment, Detective Jack Wildy, police officers, and the Chief of Police arrived on the scene and started questioning spectators. Janet went up to them and told them what she witnessed. She also mentioned that she found it rather strange that the bodies of the sailors disintegrated into ashes.

The tall, dark, and stout Chief of Police, Bill Grady, seemed distracted. His black hair stuck to his head as if plastered with grease. He barely spoke and looked fidgety. He darted his steel gray eyes from side to side and kept frowning.

After hearing what Janet said, Detective Jack Wildy went on stage to search for clues.

He discovered a false head at the back of the stage. He examined it and saw the gadgets inside it. There were gadgets for 'Attack Mode,' 'Normal,' and 'No activity.' The 'No activity' mode was switched on for the false head. How could this be when it was clear that the sailors were all in 'Attack Mode'? He also observed that a number was inscribed inside the head. It was Number Nine. He placed the head in his evidence bag and whispered something to the Chief of Police, who nodded his head.

WAS NINE A ZOMBIE HERO?

Janet arrived at the hospital in disarray. She was not dressed for work. She dashed into her office and threw on her doctor's coat. Raynor walked by and saw that she was visibly shaken. He said, "Janet, I thought that you were off today. Your secretary told me that you were taking your Mom and sisters to the Carnival celebrations. You look upset. Is something wrong?"

"Raynor, I would love to tell you all about it, but we have a hospital full of people with injuries from the carnival celebrations. They need our services. Will you help if you have no babies to deliver?"

"So that's it? There was an explosion or something? You were there. Is that why you appear so shaken? Sure I will help."

"Yes. The patients will tell you more about it. Let's go to the emergency unit."

Together they hurried to the emergency unit. Other doctors and dozens of nurses were already attending to the injured who were relating what took place at the Arena. Dr. Mark Schmidt and Dr. George Brown rushed to the emergency ward to help.

The news of the tragedy spread throughout the island like wildfire and made world news headlines on television. Newspaper and television reports stated that it was a terrorist attack on the island in the middle of their jubilant carnival celebrations.

Meanwhile, the Chief of Police, assisted by Detective Jack Wildy, searched vigilantly for more clues to solve the vicious crime. They assigned many senior police officers to help with the case.

Based on the conversation he had with Dr. George Brown and Dr. Raynor Sharpe, Jack Wildy had already formed his conclusions, which he kept to himself. He needed more to go on before disclosing his findings. He called both doctors to the police station the following day to discuss what he had found.

When the doctors arrived at the station, they were ushered to a secluded area where the Chief of Police and Detective Jack Wildy sat. "I have good news and bad news," said Jack Wildy to them. "Have a seat."

He raised the false head above his head. "Recognize this, Dr. Brown?" he asked.

"Where did you get that?" said Dr. Brown.

"I found this on the stage at the Carnival Arena after the massacre. Do you know what is written inside of it? Number Nine."

"I know that false head. It was the one that Number Nine had on when he visited me. Is he involved in this crime?" asked Dr. Brown.

"He and fifty others. They paraded as a jolly sailor band at the Carnival celebrations. Their one intention was to kill and maim as many as they could, and they succeeded," said Jack.

"So Number Nine told Dr. Brown the truth. It means that Master Zeeka, whoever he is, is behind all of this. Did you all ever find him?" asked Raynor.

"The elusive Master Zeeka has not yet been found, but our men are searching for him. There is more. Look at these gadgets inside the head. There are gadgets for 'Attack Mode,' 'Normal,' and 'No activity.'

The 'No activity' mode was switched on for Number Nine when the other fifty sailors were obviously all in 'Attack Mode.'

It seems that someone was controlling these zombies using a transponder. I suspect it was Zeeka, whoever he is.

The other sailors were the brothers he spoke of in the conversation with you. The strangest thing is that after the police had killed them, they fell to the ground, and seconds later, their bodies disintegrated into ash. There was no trace of human matter. I found this head a few feet away from the stage as if its owner flung it there on purpose.

We have a witness too. It is one of your doctors, Dr. Janet Jones. The good news is that I believe you, Dr. Brown. There was a Number Nine, and he spoke the truth. He said that he did not agree with killing people and he was not a bad person.

It seems that he deliberately threw out that false head to send a message to us that he was not responsible for killing anyone. He was indeed a hero, a zombie hero if I must say.

The bad news is that we cannot find Zeeka. It is alleged that Zeeka is Dr. Jason Stephens, and we have no evidence yet to prove that. We assure you that we have arranged a manhunt to find him and interrogate him.

The body count that day was one hundred and twenty-five. He may or may not be responsible for killing those people. Seventy-five people were seriously injured, and they are still in the hospital. By the way, the Government official who assisted Zeeka in getting the stillborn babies before burial passed away five years ago."

At that point, the Chief of Police, who was not a man of many words, interjected. "We want to thank you both for bringing the matter of Number Nine to our attention in the first place. Your assistance will help us to solve this heinous crime and bring the real perpetrator to justice. We will keep in touch. Thanks again for coming."

THE WEDDING INVITATION

George and Raynor returned to the hospital satisfied that the investigations were heading in the right direction. Jack Wildy had tied up many loose ends, but the main suspect was still at large. Raynor told Mark all about the discussions with Jack Wildy. They returned to their routine at the hospital. A few days passed.

One week later Raynor had just finished seeing his last patient and was packing up to head home for a good night's rest. He opened his desk drawer to get his car keys and saw Janet's wedding invitation lying there. He took it up to take it home.

His thoughts led him back to the first day she came to work at the hospital. She was young, beautiful, and intelligent. He never felt the way he felt about her for any other woman. He tried to dismiss the thought. She was getting married to someone else. *"Why can't I get her off my mind?"* he said shaking his head and sighing.

Mark Schmidt walked in the door. “Did you open it yet?” he shouted.

“What?” Raynor asked.

“Did you open the wedding invitation?”

“No. I am taking it home,” Raynor replied, as he stood up to leave.

“For God’s sake open it now Raynor,” Mark said in a high-pitched voice.

“Mark are you in love with her too?”

“No Raynor, just open the invitation now.”

“All right, Mark. Is there a bomb in here?” he joked as he ripped open the envelope.

Raynor could not believe his eyes as he read the invitation. His jaw dropped as he read,

Dr. Janet Jones and Dr. Jason Stephens request the honour of your presence to witness their marriage on Sunday, 30th March 2036 at five o’clock in the afternoon, at the Hyatt Resort, 23 Palms Road, Lakeville, Gosh. RSVP

Raynor dropped back down on his chair in shock. He took up the phone to call Jack Wildy. He suddenly thought, could Janet be involved with Jason’s revenge plan?

He dropped the phone, looked up at Mark, and asked, “Do you think that Janet is criminally involved with him or is Stephens using her as part of his revenge plan?”

“No Raynor. Do you know what I feel? I think that she’s in love with you, and she agreed to go along with marriage to someone else, to test your reaction. I do not believe she knows that Jason Stephens is a vicious criminal.”

“Mark, we have to save Janet from the claws of that devil. Will you help me?”

“Sure, I will. Nevertheless, we must inform the police. It seems that Janet alone knows where Stephens lives.”

Raynor tried to compose himself and his thoughts for a while and then said, “We should alert Dr. George Brown about this and then decide where we go from there.”

“That’s a good idea,” said Mark. “Is he available?”

“Let’s check,” said Raynor.

They both proceeded to walk towards Dr. Brown’s office.

On their way, they passed Janet's office. She was packing up to leave for the day.

She called out to them, "What's up with both of you?"

Raynor asked her, "Are you busy tonight?"

"I have a dinner date with my fiancé."

"Really," Raynor replied, trying to sound as if he was not prying. "I suppose that you are going to your favorite place."

"We're trying out the new restaurant at the Bay. I believe the name is Bay View Restaurant."

"Enjoy it," Raynor said, as he and Mark walked away not wanting to raise any suspicion of their intentions.

SEARCH ON FOR STEPHENS

Dr. Brown was sitting in his office reading electronic files on the hospital's monitor as Mark and Raynor entered.

"You both look serious. What's wrong?" he asked.

"Did Janet invite you to her wedding on 30th March?" Mark asked Dr. Brown.

"Yes she did, but I'll not be available on that date. I'll not be attending."

"Did you read the invitation?" Raynor asked.

"My secretary noted the date in my tablet," he said, swiping the pages of his tablet to find the entry.

"Do you know to whom she is getting married?" asked Mark.

"Didn't you two get invitations too? I did not read mine. My secretary handled that and replied that I am unable to attend," said Dr. Brown looking annoyed.

“Have a look at this.” Raynor handed his invitation to George. He took it and glanced at it.

“What’s wrong with it? It is a typical wedding invitation.”

George’s eye suddenly caught the names on the invitation, and he exclaimed, “My God. Does Janet know about this mass murderer? We have to warn her.”

“Yes, we have to tell her about him. She said that she’s meeting him for dinner at Bay View Restaurant tonight,” said Mark.

“We’ll go there and take Jack Wildy with us. We have to nail him tonight,” said George. “I’ll contact Jack. Both of you should go ahead and change. Try to get there before 7.00 pm.”

“See you later,” Raynor said.

All four arrived at the restaurant at 6.45 pm, but neither Janet nor Dr. Jason Stephens was in sight. They ordered drinks and dinner and waited anxiously for the couple’s arrival.

At 8.00 pm, Janet walked in alone and sat at a table with her back turned to the group of four. She could not see them, but they could see her. At 8.30 pm, Jason had not yet arrived.

At 9.00 pm, there was still no sign of him, and Janet seemed restless. She appeared to be constantly texting on her phone. She then took up her purse and stormed out of the restaurant.

Jack Wildy said, “Maybe Dr. Jason Stephens knows that the police are on to him, and he has absconded.”

“I agree,” said Dr. Brown. “Now who will pay for all the havoc he caused on Carnival Monday? He deserves to get the death sentence for killing all those innocent people and causing injury to many others.”

“When we find him he’ll get what he deserves, “said Jack.

They left the restaurant after a quick meal and a couple of beers.

Raynor could not get Janet off his mind. He wanted to see her and to find out why her dinner date was cancelled. He decided to swing by her house to see if she was at home. Sure enough, her car was parked in the driveway. He got out of his car, walked up to her door and knocked. After a few seconds, Janet looked out of the bedroom window.

She recognized him standing at the door and ran down the staircase to open it. "What are you doing here?"

"I was in the neighborhood and decided to check up on you."

"I was about to go to bed, but you can come in for a cup of coffee."

"Are you sure?"

"To be honest, Raynor, I need company right now. Come inside."

It was the first time Raynor saw Janet's home. It was quite neat, attractively laid out, and appeared quite cozy.

He sat on a comfortable-looking chair and Janet went to bring out the coffee. Raynor decided that was the ideal opportunity to search for photos of Dr. Jason Stephens. He got up and looked around, but there were no pictures of him. Janet walked in with the coffee and blurted out, "I may as well tell you. I'm calling off the wedding."

"What? Why the sudden change of heart?" said Raynor trying not to sound too excited.

"My fiancé never turned up for our dinner date. He never answered my calls, and when I went to his home, the house was empty. There was a note for me with just three words, 'Forget me, Janet.' She was almost in tears. "I destroyed all photos of us. How could he forsake me two weeks before our wedding, and without any explanation? I'll never forgive him for the embarrassment he has caused me."

Raynor saw that she was extremely upset and heart-broken. He did not have the heart to tell her what he knew. He decided to wait until the next day to break the news to her. He spent a few minutes with her trying to comfort her and then left.

JANET AND RAYNOR MARRY

The following day, Raynor woke up late and arrived at the hospital one hour late for work. When he reached the hospital, he went to Janet's office to see how she was doing. He saw Detective Jack Wildy and Dr. George Brown speaking to her. Janet looked at him as he arrived and said, "You knew all of this all along and never told me anything?"

Raynor suddenly realized that they were telling her the truth about Jason Stephens. "I only found out the name of your fiancé yesterday when I read the wedding invitation. Last night, I could not bear to tell you the truth because you were very upset when he stood you up at the restaurant. I was coming to talk to you about it this morning."

Janet said, "With friends like you, who needs enemies?"

She turned to Jack Wildy and said, "If Jason ever tries to contact me again I'll find out where he is hiding and report to you. I'm so glad that the truth was discovered before I went ahead with the wedding."

Jack Wildy was getting up from the chair to leave when he suddenly remembered something. He said, “Last night we found Dr. Stephens’ house and searched it. Do you know what we found? We found the missing file of the scientist who died in a fire in Africa years ago.

There is a connection between that scientist and Dr. Jason Stephens. Maybe he was the one responsible for killing that scientist and stealing his files. We still have not found that underground hideout, nor Dr. Stephens, and that is worrying. I fear for the safety of all of you, but I have my men working 24/7 on the case.”

Janet looked stunned on hearing that. Detective Wildy and Dr. George Brown then left Janet’s office, but Raynor remained. He said to her, “Janet, I’m sorry.”

Before Raynor finished the sentence, Janet said, “I do not blame you or anyone else, Raynor. I’m a fool to allow myself to be tricked by such a scoundrel. I’ll just cancel all plans for the wedding.” She turned around to read her patients’ files from the monitor behind her.

Raynor could not believe that the words flowed from his lips so smoothly, “Janet, if you will agree to marry me, there will be no need to cancel the wedding plans."

Janet was quiet. She turned around slowly and saw a sparkling diamond engagement ring in Raynor's hand. Raynor looked most sincere. "Raynor, if you had asked me to marry you nine years ago, I would have said yes. It isn't even nine minutes since you asked me." She stopped speaking for a few seconds. "My answer is still yes." She ran into his arms, and they hugged and kissed.

By that time, nurses and doctors who had heard Raynor's proposal had gathered around and started clapping.

The spectacular wedding took place on 30th March 2036 at the Hyatt Resort in the presence of one hundred guests, just as Janet had originally planned. Mark Schmidt was the best man, and one of Janet's sisters was the matron of honour. Janet looked radiant in a white floor-length traditional bridal gown made of lace and tuille with a long flowing train. She carried a bridal bouquet of red roses, which were her favorite flowers. Her matron of honour wore a royal blue floor-length dress of lace.

After the couple had exchanged their vows, there was a banquet dinner, followed by the cutting of the six-tiered cake. Each tier was made in a different flavour. Dancing followed, but the couple was anxious to leave the celebrations to go on their honeymoon.

Raynor surprised Janet with a honeymoon that she had always dreamt of. They flew halfway across the world, and then hopped on a private sailboat that took them to a secluded island where they were greeted with champagne and freshly cut fruit.

They had an unforgettable honeymoon on the island. They both realized that their love for each other was stronger than they imagined. Their time alone together flew, and they returned to Gosh to start their lives as husband and wife. Janet moved in with Raynor in his beachfront home, and they got back into the routine of their daily lives.

Jason Stephens remained at large. Would Jack Wildy and his team ever find him?

Read the other books in the series to find out more.

BOOKS IN THIS SERIES

1. Zeeka and the Zombies
2. Zeeka's Child
3. Zeeka Returns
4. Zeeka's Ghost
5. Resurrection
6. Zeeka Chronicles -Five series – adapted into a screenplay.
7. Revenge of Zeeka Trilogy - three series
8. Zeeka and the Zombies II - Four –Series, which has been adapted into a screenplay, and placed in the finals of the 13Horror-com Film & Screenplay Contest in September 2025.

REVIEW FOR ZEEKA CHRONICLES

Reviewed by Sarah Stuart for Readers' Favorite International.

Zeeka Chronicles: Revenge of Zeeka [Five – Series] by Brenda Mohammed opens with Zeeka and the Zombies. On the island of Gosh in January 2036, Raynor Sharpe is woken by rattling to find a beach full of small robots. Is he still dreaming? Raynor is a hospital doctor, and so is the woman he secretly loves, but Janet is engaged to another man. Gosh's carnival is turned from an exotic native spectacle to tragedy by a troop of entertainers: zombies who shoot into the audience, killing and injuring hundreds. How can these monsters disintegrate into a heap of dust? Why is one false head found? Who is Zeeka, and does he control the zombies? Why does Janet cancel her wedding? Can the Chief of Police be trusted, or is he as corrupt as others in the force? Read on: Zeeka's Child, Zeeka Returns, Zeeka's Ghost, and Resurrection hold the un-guessable answers.

Zeeka Chronicles comprises five books from the Revenge of Zeeka series in which 2036 is shown as a technically advanced world by gadgets like watches that act much like today's smartphones, plus visual contact, robots, and much more. The story is built on the premise that a doctor discovers a cure for a disease, but is prevented from using it. However, the plot becomes more entangled the farther you read, with police corruption, suicide, kidnapping, and a very active ghost. Brenda Mohammed's writing style is evocative of the future, and she handles the science in her fiction brilliantly: reading is believing! I loved Zeeka Chronicles; it has worldwide appeal for anyone looking for an entertaining story that is different."

Readers' Favorite LLC

Media Relations

Louisville, KY 40202

ZEEKA'S CHILD

Secrets, lies, human flaws, and 'skeletons in cupboards' are revealed and exposed in Zeeka's Child, the second episode of the five-book science fiction series Revenge of Zeeka.

Who is the mystery Master Zeeka and who is Zeeka's child?

In Book 1 it was assumed that Master Zeeka was a scientist. The police were searching for

Dr. Jason Stephens, but they were chasing the wrong suspect.

Quirky Detective Jack Wildy and his counterpart Jerry Cole join the investigation into the Massacre of innocent people by zombies at the Carnival event.

Detective Jack Wildy discovers a flash drive revealing the face of the real perpetrator.

Dr. Jason Stephens gives another flash drive to Janet to deliver to Dr, Raynor Sharpe, confirming Wildy's discovery, and about the child Master Zeeka kidnapped.

Extract of a Review by an ardent fan.

"The second book answers many questions the first book left us with, but it also poses many new questions.

That's why I am already looking forward to reading the third book.

I read this book in one sitting since it's difficult to put down once one starts to read it.

The story itself is quite complex for such a short book.

There are not many authors who can say so much without wasting a single word.

Brenda Mohammed excels in this respect."

ZEEKA RETURNS

Action, adventure, high-tech weapons, zombies, and robots in Zeeka Returns, the third book in the five-book science fiction series Revenge of Zeeka: will keep you on the edge of your seat.

Sixty programmable zombies with one sinister goal in mind, 'to seek and destroy' deepen the suspense and drama of the story.

The continuing manhunt in the forest for Zeeka and his zombies makes this book a thrilling read.

Zeeka abandons his zombies in the forest and goes to the home of Dr. Raynor Sharpe to look for his brother, Steven, who is staying there temporarily.

Janet's helper, Miranda, a beautiful robot, uses her taekwondo skills to capture Zeeka after seeing him holding a gun. She saves the police a lot of trouble.

Read how the police shrink zombies and demolish them with high-tech weapons.

Reviewer:

"If you enjoyed the first two, this book is a must. The story of Zeeka's twisted mind continues to amaze us.

Definite movie possibilities here."

ZEEKA'S GHOST

What happens when a strong wind throws down Zeeka's urn and it falls and breaks, his ashes scatter in Steven's study, and Zeeka's ghost appears to Dr. Steven Sharpe whom Zeeka had kidnapped as a child?

The drama of the Zeeka Series continues in Zeeka's Ghost: Revenge of Zeeka Book 4.

Can dead people return to Earth to make amends?

The ghost begs for forgiveness from Steven and saves Mandy, Steven's wife, from dangerous kidnappers.

Read a review from a fan.

'Extending from her Zeeka and the Zombies trilogy is Mohammed's fourth book in the Revenge of Zeeka Series, a most nostalgic offering, Zeeka's Ghost.

Zeeka is back, but not at all how you expect.

Unresolved issues, regrets, and love are all splendidly woven together with the right mix of startling plot twists the author is masterful at.

Fans of the series will not be disappointed and new fans will be caught up to speed in no time.

Another thrilling read! '

RESURRECTION

Resurrection: Revenge of Zeeka Book 5 is the grand finale in the mind-boggling five-book Science fiction series Revenge of Zeeka. Someone resurrected and it is not Zeeka.

Number Nine, the zombie, who police thought was dead in the massacre at the Carnival event in February 2036 is alive.

Mandy's robot helper, Eve, encounters a stranger in the backyard.

When Eve tells him she is a robot, he tells her his story. Eve promises to keep their discussion a secret, but records the conversation on her security device and plays it for Steven and Mandy.

Number Nine collapses in the backyard with an epileptic fit, and Eve alerts the Gosh hospital. Tests and records confirm that he is Number Nine. He is not a zombie and is the biological son of Bill Grady – Master Zeeka, who made him grow up with zombies because he was misdiagnosed with microcephaly- a disease associated with the zika virus that infected his mother, Angelina Grady, who died in childbirth. His name is Nieman Grady and is 22 years old.

Steven faces opposition to the launch of his most significant invention of the century.

Nieman Grady - Number Nine is the first volunteer to test it and is healed of his neurological disorder.

Here is an extract from a review.

'While the series started with possible abuse of medical technology, the last book leaves us hopeful that technology can one day serve us better than most of us can imagine.'

REVIEW FOR ZEEKA AND THE ZOMBIES II

ZEEKA AND THE ZOMBIES II, a gripping sci-fi horror novel, was adapted into a four-series screenplay and was selected as a finalist in the 13Horror-com Film & Screenplay Contest 2025.

The futuristic sci-fi horror thriller written by Trinidadian Brenda Mohammed, who has published 68 books to date, was selected among the top 25% of entries.

The feature-length screenplay based on this novel was praised by judges for its genre-defying fusion of futuristic sci-fi, Caribbean folklore, and dark fantasy, set in a vividly imagined 2036 Caribbean Island.

Andrew Hannon, the Contest Director and one of the Hollywood judges, commended the screenplay for its complex narrative, emotional depth, and cinematic horror, highlighting standout moments such as the Carnival massacre, the twist involving Chief of Police Bill Grady, and the poignant revelation of Zeeka's hidden humanity.

A psychotic cop, who has adopted the alias MASTER ZEEKA, unleashes a horde of zombies upon a Caribbean paradise amidst its carnival festivities. It's up to two long-separated brothers, with a surprising connection to the cop, to save the day.

The sci-fi horror novel is loaded with several twisty thrills and intriguing revelations. The brothers Dr. Raynor Sharpe and Dr. Steven Sharpe, a malicious zombie horde, two detectives, and Master Zeeka, who created the zombies, are the main characters of the novel.

Number Nine, the zombie who discovered he was not a zombie, but just struggling with a strange illness, is cured by Dr. Steven Sharpe with a Miracle Machine he invented.

Readers of Caribbean sci-fi horror and zombie fiction will love this story.

REVENGE OF ZEEKA HORROR TRILOGY

Reviewed by Faridah Nassozi for Readers' Favorite

In Revenge of Zeeka by Brenda Mohammed, the island of Gosh is under attack by an army of zombies under the command of a vengeful science genius. In the year 2016, the Zika virus broke out in Central and South America with life-threatening effects on pregnant women.

Given a choice to save the mothers or the unborn babies, a decision was made to save the mothers. The tiny stillborns were securely and secretly buried.

Only a few people knew of this. Unknown to everyone, however, a certain scientist managed to get hold of all 51 bodies, bring them back to life, and condition them to follow his command, creating himself a perfect army of zombies.

Now, twenty years later, the evil scientist seeks revenge on those he holds responsible for the stillbirths. Only three of the current doctors at Central Hospital - Raynor, Mark, and George - witnessed the unfortunate events of 2016. The three have strong suspicions about who might be controlling the zombies.

Meanwhile, Zeeka is lying in wait for the perfect time to unleash his army onto the island. Zeeka has big, evil plans and this is just the beginning. In a desperate search for answers, and with very little to go on, the doctors search for the elusive Master Zeeka.

Will they save the islanders from Zeeka and his zombies, or will it be too late?

Revenge of Zeeka by Brenda Mohammed is a one-of-a-kind novella trilogy that delivers an incredible story guaranteed to give readers an absolute sci-fi treat. I especially liked how Brenda used current events as the pivotal point from which to build this amazing sci-fi horror.

This made the story even more relatable. More importantly, however, I admired how she owned her story and created this captivating version of events.

She captured with amazing depth the setting, characters, plot, and emotions in such few words.

If you are looking for a thrilling short read, this fast-paced, sci-fi action novella will give you the time of your life.

ABOUT THE AUTHOR

Brenda Mohammed is a prolific, multi-award-winning author and screenwriter from Trinidad and Tobago. She has published 68 books and 68 audiobooks across diverse genres, including science fiction, memoirs, mystery, romance, psychological thrillers, Christian non-fiction, children's books, self-help, poetry, and three screenplays.

Her acclaimed sci-fi thriller, Zeeka Chronicles, has been adapted into a five-series screenplay.

Her four-series sci-fi horror, Zeeka and the Zombies, was a finalist in the 13Horror.com Film & Screenplay Contest.

Additionally, her suspense romance, The Gift of Love, advanced to the quarterfinals of Stage 32 and Drama Box competitions.

Her work was featured in USA News and BIZWEEKLY in 2025.

In 2021, Alem Hailu of the Ethiopian Herald published an interview with her in the Sunday issue.

INTERNATIONAL LITERARY AWARDS

1. After surviving a near-fatal battle with cancer, she wrote I AM CANCER FREE, a bestselling memoir that won an award in the Reader's Favorite International Awards 2018.

2. Her gripping five-series futuristic Caribbean sci-fi thriller, ZEEKA CHRONICLES, won an award in the Reader's Favorite International Awards 2018, and also won an award in Science Fiction in SIBA Awards 2017, won the gold award in the category Science Fiction in Connections Emagazine Readers' Choice Awards 2018, and was a winner in the top ten finalists for

science fiction in the Author Academy Global Awards 2018.

3 Her romance novel, THE GIFT OF LOVE, has also been adapted into a short screenplay for television and made it to the Quarterfinals of the Stage 32 Drama Box Screenwriting Competition in April 2026.

4. Her memoir, MY LIFE AS A BANKER, won second place for 'best memoir' in the Metamorph Publishing Summer Indie Book Awards 2016.

5. Her self-help guide, HOW TO WRITE FOR SUCCESS I, was hailed by the Ethiopian Herald as "a comprehensive toolkit for writers, critics, and editors." In August 2019, the book topped all books in the Non-Fiction category of the Connections Emagazine Readers' Choice awards and won the gold medal. It also placed second in all categories and won the silver medal. It was a triple victory for Brenda, because her romance novel, 'STORIES PEOPLE LOVE,' placed first in all categories and won the gold medal.

6. BARRY HOLMES MYSTERIES received a five-star review from Readers' Favorite International in September 2021, won the Culture, Literature, and Research [CLR]

Award in India for Best Writer- Fantasy, received a certificate of recognition from The International Chamber of Writers and Artists [CIESART], Spain in 2023 on World Book Day, and was a finalist in the Independent Author Awards 2024 hosted by Literary Global Awards.

Literary Network:

She founded the "How to Write for Success" Facebook forum, where she actively mentors writers and hosts poetry contests.

Leadership & Community Roles

CIESART: Since 2022, she has been appointed National Delegate and President of the International Chamber of Writers and Artists, headquartered in Spain, and is involved in charity, culture, and Art.

Local Advocate:

She has hosted local book fairs, including successful book signings at Gulf View Mall in San Fernando, and she frequently advocates for World Peace, suicide prevention, domestic violence, drug addiction, and human trafficking prevention through the publication of several Anthologies.

To explore her extensive catalogue or follow her latest updates, visit the official Brenda Mohammed Author website at https://brenchristo.com.

BOOKS BY AUTHOR

CHILDREN'S BOOKS

2014 - Adventures of Squeaky Doo– Five exciting travel Memoirs of a Teddy Bear that children love.

2017 - She Cried for Me – the heart-wrenching autobiography of a stray dog. The book is also available in Audio.

2020 -The Child Poet – A poetic Galaxy for Children, was a hot new release within hours of being published. A No 1 hot new release.

FICTION THRILLERS

2021 -The Manipulator: A Psychological Thriller - This thriller will have you holding on to your seat with your eyes glued to its pages.

2021 – Conspiracy Stories – Within this book, you'd find three chilling and addictive stories to awaken your mind.

MYSTERY THRILLERS

2018 - The Gift of Love: Barry Holmes Mysteries Book 1 – a crime fiction/romance. A No 1 bestseller.

2019 - The Axe Murderer: Barry Holmes Mysteries Book 2 – a crime fiction highlighting kidnapping for ransom.

2020 - What happened to Mary Loo: Barry Holmes Mysteries Book 3 – a suspense-filled mystery about a businesswoman who mysteriously disappeared just after the CoVid 19 lockdown.

2020 - Barry Holmes Mysteries: Tales of Mysterious Disappearances – Three mind-blowing tales of mystery.

MEMOIRS

2013 - I am Cancer Free: A Memoir – the true story of the author's miraculous recovery from cancer.

2014 - Memoirs of Dr. A. M. Khan: Journey of an Educator – gives a glimpse into life in the days of Indentureship in Trinidad and Tobago.

2014 - My Life as a Banker: A Life Worth Living – a motivational memoir of Brenda's life in the banking sector.

2014- Retirement is Fun: A new Chapter – filled with travel adventures after the author moved on from a banking career.

2014 - Travel Memoirs with Pictures: Exploring the world – a pictorial memoir of the author's travels around the world.

CHRISTIAN BOOKS

2014 - Your Time Is Now: A Time to be Born and a Time to Die – gives answers to compelling questions.

2022 – He is the One: A book for End Times. This book gives answers about eternal life. A No 1 hot new release.

2022- Chosen by the Creator: Bible Stories

CHRISTIAN POETRY

Highway to Joy Eternal - a book of poetic verses with encouraging and inspiring messages of hope and love.

True Power of Love - a book of poetic verses about the miracles performed by Jesus Christ, which were beyond the reach of human action and natural causes.

God-Fearing Ones - motivational poems for readers who struggle to read the Bible regularly.

Keys to Withstand the Storms of Life - poems to give readers hope in a life full of struggles.

Now is the Time to Prepare - a series of poetry compiled by the author to enlighten readers on future events.

Christmas Messages - poems about the Greatest Gift that God gave to humankind.

POETRY TO INSPIRE

2019 - Strength for the Disheartened: Motivational Poems – a collection of poems to motivate and inspire.

2019 - Dreams of the Heart: A Poetry Collection – a selection of several unique poems for romantic poetry lovers.

2020 - A Road Travelled: Poetry to Delight – the book features a wide range of inspirational poems on Love, Love's woes, Travel, Happiness, and effects on life during lockdown at the time of CoVid 19.

2020 - Soothing Poetry in English and Spanish - The poems are didactic, fun to read, and full of hope and insight. A No 1 bestseller.

2020 - Chaotic Times: Poetry Vaccine for Covid 19 published jointly with Florabelle Lutchman. A No 1 bestseller.

2020 – Sweet Medley: A Poetic Joy contains a medley of poems by Author Brenda Mohammed on varied subjects of life, love, and nature. A No 1 bestseller.

2021 – Just for You: Poetic Flowers – contains poems of love, childhood, and sundry thoughts, as well as Love poems. A No 1 bestseller.

2021 – Truth - Both poetry and prose within this book are about truth. A No 1 bestseller.

2021 – Teatime Poetry - A collection of different styles of poetry. A No 1 bestseller.

2021 – Treasured Memories – A collection of travel poems that will motivate readers to achieve more in life. A No 1 bestseller.

2021 – Islands in the Sun – Poetic verses about Trinidad and Tobago, the author's homeland. A No 1 hot new release.

2024 – Save God's Earth – Poems on Climate Change

2024 - Beauty of Poetry – Poems to forget Sorrows

ROMANCE

2014 - Stories People Love– Six exciting short stories of crime, adventure, and love. The stories are very alluring.

2014 - Heart-Warming Tales– Six thrilling and suspenseful tales of Crime, Love, and Unhappy Marriages. A No 1 bestseller.

2019 - Stories that Intrigue - a romance novel, contains the love story of Sam and Julia.

SCIENCE FICTION

2016 - Zeeka and the Zombies: Revenge of Zeeka Book 1 –the first book in a spine-chilling science fiction series and a No 1 best seller.

2016 - Zeeka's Child: Revenge of Zeeka Book 2– Mystery surrounds the birth of Zeeka's Child.

2016 - Zeeka Returns: Revenge of Zeeka Book 3– Zeeka decides his fate.

2016 - Revenge of Zeeka: Horror Trilogy comprises the first three stories in the award-winning series Revenge of Zeeka.

2016 - Zeeka's Ghost: Revenge of Zeeka Book 4– Zeeka's Ghost haunts Steven.

2017 - Resurrection: Revenge of Zeeka Book 5– the sudden appearance of a stranger, bothers Steven.

2017 - Zeeka Chronicles: Revenge of Zeeka: This multi-award-winning science-fiction novel, set in the year 2036, and inspired by the recent scare of the zika virus, where zombies and robots take center stage, has won four awards.

2025 – Zeeka and the Zombies – Four series

SELF-HELP

2017 - How to Write for Success: Best Writing Advice I Received – a popular guide for new and aspiring authors. A No 1 bestseller.

2021 – How to Write for Success: Volume Two. The book focuses on publishing and marketing.

2022 – Self Publishing Tips

POETRY ANTHOLOGIES

2019 – A Spark of Hope 1 co-authored by 49 authors, is a No 1 bestseller in Poetry Anthologies for the prevention of suicide.

2020 - A Spark of Hope 2 coauthored by 64 authors, is also a No 1 bestseller in Poetry Anthologies for the prevention of suicide.

2023 – A Spark of Hope 3

2020 –Break the Silence, coauthored by 84 authors, is a No 1 bestseller in Poetry Anthologies against domestic violence.

2021- Break the Silence: Volume Two coauthored by 91 authors is a No 1 bestseller in Poetry Anthologies, Inspirational and Religious Poetry, and a No 1 Hot new release.

2025 – Break The Silence III

MAGAZINES

March 2021 - How to Write for Success Literary Magazine: Anniversary Issue. A No 1 bestseller.

Sept 2021- How to Write for Success: Literary magazine - Second Issue. A No 1 bestseller.

February 2022 – How to Write for Success Literary Magazine – Third Issue. A No 1 bestseller.

2024 – How to Write for Success Literary Magazine

2025 – How to Write for Success Literary Magazine

CIESART HUMMING BIRD MAGAZINES

2022, 2023, 2024, 2025

HUMMING BIRD is an annual magazine of the International Chamber of Writers and Artists [CIESART] – Trinidad and Tobago.

Within the contents, you will find exquisite poetry collections and articles composed by key individuals, including the President, Vice President, and Director, who collaborated to compile the magazine.

COPYRIGHT NOTICE

ZEEKA AND THE ZOMBIES I

Published 21st. February 2016

Updated 17th July 2026

www.ingramcontent.com/pod-product-compliance
Lightning Source LLC
LaVergne TN
LVHW031344150826
845673LV00009B/2860

* 9 7 8 1 5 2 0 6 1 4 5 8 8 *